Jet Black
Heart

TERESA FLAVIN

First published in 2014 in Great Britain by
Barrington Stoke Ltd
18 Walker Street, Edinburgh, EH3 7LP

www.barringtonstoke.co.uk

Text and Illustrations © 2014 Teresa Flavin

A CIP catalogue record for this book is available
from the British Library upon request

ISBN: 978-1-78112-404-8

Printed in China by Leo

For Maddie, Leanne and Camille

CHAPTER 1

It happened so fast there was nothing Dory could do. One minute she was running down the hillside trying to catch up with her sister Gracie. The next minute Dory tripped so hard, the world flipped over and she tumbled down the rest of the hill, unable to stop herself.

Dory landed on flat mossy ground and lay there, stunned. After a moment she found she could move her arms and legs. She didn't seem to have broken anything, but the palms of her hands stung and she had a painful graze on one knee.

"Gracie?" she called, in a feeble voice. "Gracie!" But all she heard was the tinkle of a stream close by.

Dory and her sister were on a kind of treasure hunt called letter-boxing.

"Letter-boxing is really popular here," Dad had said when he handed Gracie the clue map that morning. "You'll have a great time."

Yeah, right. What you did was search for hidden plastic boxes with a map. When you found one, you took out the rubber stamp inside and used it to stamp a notebook. It was tragic. Things like that were for little kids and geeks like Gracie. But Dad and Mum wouldn't let Dory out of it. Gracie had called her a misery and they had bickered all the way along the Crake Ridge cliff path until they arrived at some stone steps.

The letter-boxing map showed that the steps led down into a wood, then a beach cove. Gracie had pushed past Dory and raced down the steps. That was when Dory had decided to take a shortcut down the hillside and sneak up on her sister. But it was Dory who had got a shock, not Gracie. Dory called again. "Gracie, I'm here! I've hurt my knee!" There was still no answer and Dory's anger rose. This was all Gracie's fault and she would laugh her head off at Dory lying in the dirt. That thought was enough to make Dory take a deep breath and push herself up to a sitting position.

One of her knees was skinned raw, but at least there was no blood. She grabbed hold of a large tree root and hauled herself up, and straight away she stubbed her toe on something hard.

There was a big old jam jar half buried under ferns below a moss-covered tree. Dory dug it out, brushed the bugs and snails off the pale greenish glass and saw something inside. When at last she managed to pull out the cork stopper, a fragile rectangle of card fell to the ground. The handwriting on it was faded but Dory could just make it out –

'Dearest Eli, I cannot wait for the day that we escape ...'

Before Dory could finish the first line, the air shimmered around her and somehow the light seemed less bright. The woods seemed denser and the ferns taller.

Even the card in Dory's hand felt different. She looked at the writing again and drew in a sharp breath. The card was now thick and crisp, the ink deep black as if it had just been written.

Somewhere behind her, a male voice spoke.

"Miss Rachel," it said. "I never thought I'd see you again."

CHAPTER 2

Spooked, Dory dropped the card and hobbled away as fast as she could, almost in tears at the pain in her knee. She snatched up a broken stick and whirled round.

A boy stood by the mossy tree, staring at Dory. He was about 17 and dressed in an old-fashioned shirt and waistcoat, dusty brown jacket and trousers that hung loose on his lean frame. His thick hair was the colour of fox fur.

The boy watched her without blinking, as if she were an animal he didn't want to startle. Dory stared back. Was he one of those arty guys that only dressed in vintage stuff? His clothes were scruffy but he was gorgeous. Still, he could be a weirdo. Dory gripped the stick harder.

The boy put his hands up. "I'm very sorry to startle you, Miss. My name is Eli and I mean you no harm."

His words were warm but Dory's skin still prickled with fear. "You scared the life out of me!" she said. "Don't come any closer."

"I do not intend to." Eli backed away. "I mistook you for someone else," he said. "Your hair is the same chestnut colour as Miss Rachel's was."

Dory wondered why he sounded so old-fashioned. He had to be putting it on. "You were spying on me," she said.

"I wasn't." Eli shook his head. "I happened to be here when you appeared."

"No, you weren't," Dory said. "I would have seen you. And what do you mean, 'appeared'?"

"You appeared out of thin air," the boy told her. "From nowhere."

Dory tensed. "Are you trying to be funny or something?"

The boy shook his head again. "Far from it."

"Where am I then, if I just 'appeared'?"

"In the same place as the one you left," said Eli. "But in another time from yours, I think. The year is 1863."

Dory drew in a sharp breath. "Oh, is that right?" she mocked. "So I'm a time-traveller? And I suppose I'm here to save Earth from a zombie attack or something. Listen, play that game with someone else. Go on, get lost."

Eli stood firm. "I know it sounds impossible but I am telling the truth, Miss," he said. "You've travelled into 1863."

"Where did you get that idea?" Dory asked. She watched his face for signs of a smirk but his expression was serious. He seemed to believe his own loony story.

"Others from the future have come and gone," he said. "Others dressed like you and Miss Rachel."

Dory decided to play along for a bit. "Gone where?" she asked.

Eli half smiled. "To where they belonged, of course."

"So I can leave too," Dory said. "Like this Miss Rachel did."

"Yes, I will show you how," Eli said. "But first, thank you for finding this." He picked up the card from among the ferns and read it. He wiped his eyes with the heel of his hand when he had finished. "I have been waiting so long for it."

He was crying. A bit of Dory's coolness melted away and she let the stick drop to her side.

"You can read it if you wish." Eli held out the card. "Then I can explain. I owe you that."

Dory remembered the first line of the card had said something about an escape. Part of her was curious, but a bigger part said no. He was still a stranger, and a weird one at that.

"Please," Eli said. "You seem very kind. I can tell you would understand."

Dory's heart beat faster at his sweet words and his gorgeous face. If she looked at him for one more second she might change her mind.

"It's nothing to do with me," she said. "I need to go. My sister will be looking for me."

"Of course," Eli said. "I've frightened you. That's the last thing I want to do." He bowed his head and put the card in his pocket. "To leave here," he said, "all you have to do is close the letter-box and put it back where you found it."

"Letter-box?" Dory echoed.

"The glass jar." Eli nodded at the jam jar. "Walkers hide them on the moors for sport and call them letter-boxes. They leave cards inside to show they were there. When other walkers come across them, they play postman and they send the cards back to those who wrote them." He shrugged. "This letter-box was empty and forgotten until I found it. So I knew it was secret and safe to use myself. But I had no idea of its power until the first visitor came."

Dory rolled her eyes. So the jar had a superpower? This was so stupid. The boy was gorgeous but he was also bonkers.

"Why do I have to put the jar back to get out of this place?" she asked, as if she believed it.

"I don't know," he said. "That's just how it is. Once you've done it you'll fade as if you were never here. And I will be alone again."

There was a catch in his voice that tugged at Dory's heart. She found herself asking, "Don't you have a family? Or friends?"

"I have not seen my family in a long time," Eli said. "And I would give anything to have one friend." He bowed and walked away. "I will leave you in peace. Goodbye, Miss."

Before Dory could say anything else, Eli vanished into the woods. She waited for a few seconds to see if he would come back with some other tale, but he didn't. A little piece of her was almost disappointed.

Dory gave the 'magic' glass jar a last glance and began to climb the hill using the stick as a support. Her friends at home were going to love this story. The only thing missing was a photo of Eli. She wished she'd taken one to show them how gorgeous he was. But Dory didn't need a photo for herself. She knew she wouldn't forget Eli in a hurry.

At the top of the hill she forgot all about photos. There was a field of long grass where the cliff path along Crake Ridge should have been. The sky was grey instead of blue. Dory shivered. "Gracie, where are you?" she called. "Gracie!"

Two men appeared at the far edge of the field. One was trying to control a huge black hound on a lead. In that moment, Dory knew Eli had told the truth. The men wore the kind of old-fashioned clothes Dory had only ever seen in costume dramas, but somehow she knew they weren't actors. This was real.

"You there!" One of the men waved at her. "Have you seen a lad with red hair round here?"

Dory heard the other man say, in an astonished voice, "She's a strange one. Dressed in boys' trousers!"

"Aye, she is," the first man said, and he stared hard at Dory. "Who are you, lass?"

Dory tried to answer but her voice wouldn't work. The hound barked and reared up.

"We're getting close, I reckon," the second man shouted. "Come on, we shall find him this time."

The dog charged towards Dory, with the men close behind. Dory screamed and half-ran, half-slid back down the hill again. She heard the dog crash towards her and she knew she wouldn't have the strength to fight it off.

All of a sudden Eli was there again. "Hurry, put this back." He placed the letter-box jar in Dory's hands and helped her to put the cork stopper back in.

As Dory pushed the jar back where she had found it, she whispered, "But what about you?"

The air shimmered and Eli was gone. Blue sky replaced the grey above the canopy of leaves. Dory curled up in a ball and hugged herself close. The summer air was warm but she trembled at the freaky stuff that had just happened. How on earth was it possible for an old jar to turn back time?

All of a sudden, Dory regretted treating Eli like he was crazy. If he hadn't been there, she would never have got back. And she hadn't even been able to thank him.

Just then Dory heard Gracie calling for her and sat up. "I'm over here!" she yelled.

"I'm coming!" her sister shouted back.

With a shaking hand, Dory pushed the bracken aside and made sure the letter-box jar was safely wedged there.

Gracie crashed through the ferns and rushed to Dory's side. Her face was creased with worry and wonder. "What happened?" she demanded. "You're white as a sheet."

"You ran off so I took a shortcut instead of the steps," Dory said. "And I fell. My new trousers are a write-off."

"Oh, no. Ouch!" Gracie kneeled down and put her arm around her sister. "I passed here a few minutes ago and didn't see you at all!" she said. "Didn't you hear me? I shouted so loud some dogs started howling." She picked leaves and moss from Dory's hair.

Dory shuddered at the thought of dogs. "I didn't hear you."

"That's weird." Gracie frowned. "Dory, you look a bit freaked out. Did anything else happen?"

Gracie was the one person who might believe Dory's story, but Dory decided to keep it to herself.

"Aliens abducted me," she said. "But they sent me back."

Gracie wrinkled her nose. "Ha ha."

"I just feel sore," Dory said. "I want to go to the B&B."

"I'll help you." Gracie hoisted her to her feet. "Come on."

Before they left Dory looked back at the spot where the letter-box jar was hidden.

Gracie followed her sister's gaze. "Why do you keep looking over there?" she asked.

Dory shook her head. "Just some rubbish I saw."

"What is it?"

"Nothing," Dory said. "Just leave it."

"OK, OK." Gracie helped Dory up the stone steps towards the cliff and the village. They passed by a posy of pink flowers tied to a fence.

"That means somebody died there, doesn't it?" Gracie asked. "Maybe they jumped over the cliff."

"Maybe," Dory said. "Cheerful thought."

Gracie squeezed Dory's arm. "I'm glad you're OK," she said. "But what happened? Is there something you're not telling me?"

"I just fell, Gracie," Dory snapped. "That's all."

"If you say so." Gracie gave her a funny look. "You don't tell me stuff any more, Dory. You've changed."

Dory let out a frustrated breath. "No, I haven't," she said. "There's nothing to tell. Why do you take everything so personally? We like different stuff. We have different friends. I don't expect you to tell me everything. I respect your privacy, Gracie. So respect mine."

Gracie ignored this. "It's because I'm only 13, isn't it?" she said. "I'm not cool enough for a 15-year-old."

"Oh, give it a rest, will you?" Dory moaned. "My knee hurts and you keep rabbiting on and on. Just leave me alone."

Dory limped towards the village in silence while Gracie sulked at her side. She couldn't get Eli's image out of her head. It seemed like a bizarre dream now, but in that short encounter they had connected. She wondered if Eli had felt it too.

Dory imagined trying to tell Mum and Dad what had happened. They wouldn't understand or believe her. She had been all ready to tell her friends at home, but now she wasn't so sure about that either. They would probably laugh at her.

No, the boy with the haunted eyes was Dory's secret. Eli. And she knew that she had to see him again.

CHAPTER 3

When they got back, Gracie headed off beachcombing and Dory went for lunch with Mum and Dad. She pushed her food around her plate and studied the letter-boxing map Gracie had left. The café was crowded with chattering people but Dory heard none of it.

"You all right, love?" Mum asked. "You've been staring at that map for ages."

"Have I?" Dory moved the map away but her gaze returned to the symbol for Scar Wood.

"I thought you weren't keen on the letter-boxing," Dad said.

Dory shrugged. "It's all right, but these days it's for kids. I heard grown-ups used to do it in the 1800s. They used to hide glass jars with messages on cards inside."

"Blimey, you had me fooled," Dad said. "You're interested after all."

Dory made a face at him. "Just kind of."

A white-haired, twinkly old man leaned across from the next table. "Sorry to stick my nose in," he said, "but I couldn't help overhearing. I'm a local history buff and know a bit about letter-boxing."

"Are any letter-boxes from the 1800s hidden around here?" Dory asked.

"Oh, yes," the man said. "People find them once in a while. Sometimes they turn up in antique shops."

Dory's pulse beat faster. "Do they ever have the cards in them?"

"Not the jars I've seen," the man said. "But I've heard of one or two with cards still in them."

"Have you ever heard about any letter-box jars in Scar Wood?" Dory asked.

"What about Scar Wood?" interrupted Gracie, who was just back from her beachcombing. She dropped a handful of stones onto their table. "I found three fossils and one piece of jet."

The man twinkled at her. "May I?" he said. He picked up the small black oval of jet and rubbed it with his thumb. "Nice piece. Did you know this is fossilised wood and it's millions of years old? I could polish it up and make it into a pendant for you."

Dory slumped in her seat, frustrated.

"That's my jewellery shop." The man pointed over his shoulder at a shop across the road. "I'm Flynn."

Dad made introductions all round, then Flynn turned back to Dory. "About your question," he said. "I don't know about letter-boxes in Scar Wood but there are plenty of tales about the place."

"Letter-boxes in Scar Wood?" Gracie repeated. "But there aren't any marked on our map."

"We know that, Gracie." Dory gave her sister a withering look. "What tales, Flynn?"

Flynn gave an over-the-top shudder. "Oh, they say Scar Wood is fine in the daytime but once the light goes ... brrr! There are lots of hidey-holes for hobgoblins to jump out at you!"

"Yeah, right." Gracie smirked. "Like hobgoblins are real."

Flynn laughed. "Maybe they are and maybe they aren't. But something's in that wood, they say."

"We saw some flowers tied on the fence on Crake Ridge," Dory said. "Who are they for?"

Flynn sighed. "A local girl went missing there many years ago," he said. "They think she must have drowned but no one knows."

"That's horrible," Dory murmured.

"Yes, it was." Flynn got to his feet. "I have to head back to the shop now," he said. "Hope to see you all again before you leave."

Dory watched a clutch of beachcombers wander along the shore as the waves rolled in towards Crake Ridge. Scar Wood was out of view behind the massive cliff. Back in 1863, men with dogs were there, hunting Eli down.

Dory pushed her chair away from the table. "I'm going for a walk," she announced.

"With that knee?" Mum asked. Gracie just shook her head and began to do a sketch in the purple-covered notebook she had brought along.

"It's OK," Dory said. "I don't want it to stiffen up."

"Where are you going?" Dad called after her.

"Just around," Dory called back. "Maybe the beach."

"No hills this time!" Mum shouted with a smile. "Get back to the B&B by 4 o'clock! Remember we're visiting that waterfall."

Dory shuffled through the winding streets of the village and joined the footpath towards Crake Ridge. She fidgeted with the new top she'd changed into. Mum said it brought out the blue of her eyes. On the other hand, her old cropped trousers brought out the colour of her bruised legs and rubbed against her bandage. She sighed. She hoped Eli would be so taken with her blue eyes he wouldn't look down at her legs.

Dory climbed down the stone steps, stopping on each one till her sore leg recovered. At the bottom she headed towards the place where she'd found the letter-box. She had the jitters when she thought about what she planned to do. Scar Wood was silent, except for the tinkling stream and the swish of the ferns. Dory had just begun to fear she'd never find the right spot again, when she came to a patch of flattened ferns and the same mossy tree. After a rummage in the bracken she found the letter-box jar.

'That's weird,' Dory thought. The jar was covered in snails and moss, as if she hadn't cleaned it off that very same morning. Stranger still, the card was back inside. The writing was faded again.

Dory smoothed her hair and fidgeted with her top one last time. All she had to do was pull out the cork and she'd see Eli again. Or would she? A load of other scary possibilities filled her head. The hunters and their dog might be waiting. Or she might end up in another time by mistake. Or the letter-box might not work again. But the worst thought was that she would never see Eli again.

She yanked the cork out.

The air shimmered and Dory watched the card's ink grow blacker. She looked around. "Eli, are you here?" she called.

There was no sign of him or anyone else. Dory's heart sank. She sat down on a tree root and read the card. Eli had said she could, hadn't he?

The card said –

Dearest Eli,

I cannot wait for the day that we escape from here. Father grows more cruel every day and he watches me all the time. He knows you have run away from Mr Hardwick's horrible school and he swears that when his men catch you he will send you to a place you'll never escape from.

He has forbidden me to leave the garden now. If you find this, it is because I managed to steal away one last time. But this is the last message I will leave in our letter-box. If I try again I am afraid they will follow me.

You must be cleverer than ever and find a way to tell me your plan. But you must get past the servants and Miss Thompson, who never lets me out of her sight.

Take care. I pray you will find a way for us to be together always.

Your loving sister,
Charlotte

Dory's horror grew as she read the card. How could a father hunt down his own son or keep him away from his sister? She saw that tears had blotted some of the words. Were they Charlotte's tears – or Eli's?

A twig snapped and Dory jumped to her feet. Eli strolled from behind a tree. His face and hair were wet. He stopped when he saw her.

"Miss," he said with a wide smile. "You've come back."

Dory's insides flipped with relief and excitement. There it was again, the feeling that something special had just clicked between them.

"My name is Dory." She tried to find the right words. "Thanks for helping me before. And I'm sorry I seemed ungrateful. I didn't believe you at first."

"Not at all. I was happy to help, Miss Dory." Eli raked back his damp hair and bowed from the waist. "And I'm very pleased to meet you."

'Miss Dory.' It didn't sound so odd coming from this boy.

"What made you return?" he asked.

Dory's cheeks went hot. "I wanted to make sure those men didn't catch you, Eli. They're hunting you, aren't they?"

"Yes. But they didn't catch me," Eli said. "And I pray they never will, Miss Dory."

"So do I," said Dory.

"That means more to me than you can know." He looked at her with a warm light in his eyes. "How are your hurt leg and hand, Miss Dory?" he asked.

Butterflies fluttered in Dory's stomach. No boy in her own time had ever looked at her that way.

"I'm better," she said. "Just a bit sore."

"I'm sorry – and I'm even more astonished that you came back," Eli said. He never took his gaze from her.

"I needed to know that you're all right," Dory said. Then she tried to calm her butterflies by changing the subject. "How long have you been here?"

Eli hesitated. "For some time. I walked for so long that I've lost track of which day is which."

"Where do you hide, Eli?"

"I have places," he said. "On the moors, by the sea, under the stars."

Dory wondered when his last meal had been. "Where do you get food and water?"

"Here and there." Eli shrugged. "Food from the sea. And I drink from the stream."

Dory held up the card from the letter-box. "This said you ran away from school." She flushed again. "Sorry ... I read it after all."

"I hoped you would," Eli said. "They call it a 'school', but it's a vile and hateful place of hunger and punishment."

"That's awful," Dory said, struck by how different their worlds were. "But don't you go home for the holidays?"

"Holidays don't exist for boys like me," said Eli. "But I don't wish to bore you, Miss Dory. I came here to fetch Charlotte's message."

"I was surprised it was back in the letter-box jar," Dory said.

"I put it there after you left," Eli told her. "It's safer than having it in my pocket. I couldn't stand to lose such a precious thing from my sister."

"So this is the only way you can talk to each other?" Dory said.

"It was, but now it is too risky," said Eli.

"How did your sister know to use the letter-box?" Dory asked.

"Charlotte and I used to hide messages in it as a game," he said. "When Father sent me away to school, I told her to look after it. When I came back, I left her a message to say I was here. We've passed a few messages back and forth since then, but it is difficult for her to come on her own."

Dory was shocked. "You mean she's been here and you didn't even see each other?"

Eli screwed his face up in frustration. "I couldn't show myself because she was with the woman my father pays to look after her. Charlotte only just managed to put the message in the jar without being spotted."

"I can't believe this is happening to you," Dory said. "It's terrible and it's so wrong. My sister and I don't always get on but I don't know what I'd do if I couldn't see her any more."

"Charlotte is the most wonderful sister anyone could have," Eli said.

Dory bit her lip. She couldn't remember the last time she had said anything positive about Gracie. "How long is it since you last saw Charlotte – I mean, in person?" she asked.

"I think she was about 10 years old," he said. "I was 15. So, two years ago."

Dory's jaw dropped. "You've been apart for two years?"

"Father kept me locked away at school. To 'make me a man', he said!" Eli clenched his fist. "I'm a disappointment to him. He would be happier if I'd never been born. Or if I died tomorrow."

Dory was horrified. "Your own father wouldn't wish for such a thing …" she murmured.

"He would," Eli said in a hollow voice. "If I died it would save him the cost of keeping me at that school. But my father can rot. I will find a way to meet Charlotte."

A cold finger of alarm shot down Dory's neck. "Hold on," she said. "How will you do that without getting caught?"

"I'll be very, very careful," Eli said. "I did sneak into the house one time, but that devil of a hound almost had me." He lifted a trouser leg to show her a circle of red bite wounds above his boot.

"Oh, Eli." Dory covered her mouth. "That's horrible. You need a doctor."

"The moment I seek a doctor they will catch me," he said.

"That bite could go septic."

Eli tossed his head. "The sea will heal it."

"I can't believe they set the dog on you. You can't go near that house again!" Dory said. "I mean it, Eli!"

Eli's voice rose. "I must see my sister, Miss Dory. She needs me. If only I could talk to her! There must be some way."

Dory looked down at the tear stains on the card. Her brain told her to wish Eli luck and to go back to her own century. But her heart swelled with pity and tenderness. "Maybe there's something I can do to help," she said.

"Well, there is ..." Eli said. "But you wouldn't want to ..."

"I wouldn't want to what?" Dory asked. "At least you could tell me that."

"There is a window in the pantry," Eli said. "The lock is broken and you can easily open it from the outside. I've tried to climb through but I'm too big." He shook his head. "No, it would not be fair to ask you."

"You think I could sneak in and talk to Charlotte?" It sounded simple when Dory put it like that. It also sounded crazy.

"I should not have mentioned it, Miss Dory." Eli sat down on a tree root and put his head in his hands. "Forget what I said."

He looked utterly alone and dejected. If Dory didn't help him, who would?

"I'll do it," she said.

"You will?" Eli looked up and fixed his hazel eyes on hers. "You are an angel, Miss Dory. It would be ..." He seemed overcome. "It would be wonderful."

Dory's insides tingled. "I just want to help," she said. "And I'm good at sneaking about."

"Then you and I are alike in that way, Miss Dory." Eli grinned.

"We can go to the house now if you want," Dory offered.

Eli smiled. "No, we need darkness on our side."

"When then?"

"Tonight." Eli seemed taller and more robust all of a sudden. "But we need to make a plan now. Come. I will show you my secret hiding place."

CHAPTER 4

"Stay behind me, Miss Dory. We must not be seen," said Eli, as they came to the edge of Scar Wood. There the stream widened into the cove before them, and flowed into the sea beyond.

"There's no one around," Dory said, as they scanned the two steep headlands on either side. Crake Ridge rose above them to the left, and extended much further into the sea than in Dory's own time. It looked like a giant's shoulder half-buried in the sea. Waves rolled towards it – lines of white spray that lit up the water like dancing ghosts.

"The beach may be busy," Eli said. He put a finger to his lips. "You'll see."

As they walked over the sand, Eli brushed away their footprints with a branch. Then the sand ran out and they were walking on crunching pebbles. The air stank of seaweed and salt and everything was under the shadow of the clouds except a sailing ship gliding along the silver line of the horizon.

A few small figures in long skirts moved along the far shore.

"We must be quick," Eli said. "The tide is coming in. Those villagers will be on their way home with jet and fossils to sell to the craftsmen in town."

Dory's head spun to think that she was in this long-lost world, with its beachcombers and sailing ships on the horizon. She wondered how many other 'visitors' from other times had been on this beach with Eli.

"Tell me about Miss Rachel," she said, feeling a slight prickle of jealousy.

Eli looked straight ahead. "She visited as you have."

"When was that?" Dory asked. "Was she from the village?"

"I don't know where Miss Rachel came from," Eli said. "She did not tell me. And I don't remember exactly when she came."

"But she was from my time?" Dory said.

"Yes," said Eli. "I believe so."

"Did you bring her here?"

Eli looked round at her. "So many questions, Miss Dory."

"Sorry," she said. "I'm just curious."

There were great stones and rocks piled up against the base of Crake Ridge.

"This way," Eli said, as he began to scramble over and around them. He reached his arm out to steady Dory. "Take care on the rocks."

As the sea came in, it tickled the furthest stones, crashing and hissing as it ebbed and flowed, but it had yet to reach them.

Eli helped Dory onto the ledge of a dark cave in the cliff face. All of a sudden a shower of pebbles pelted them from above. He pulled her into the cave and brushed off her hair and shoulders. "Are you hurt?" He was so close in the darkness that Dory could feel the heat of his body.

"No, I'm fine," she whispered.

Eli lit the stump of a candle and lifted it high, so that Dory could see the craggy cave lined in dried seaweed and broken shells. Dory held her nose as she followed him deeper inside. He stopped and aimed the candle towards a wide opening in the rock wall around the height of Dory's shoulder.

"One of my bedrooms," he said, with a short laugh that echoed through the cave. He handed Dory the candle and climbed up into the opening. "The dog cannot pick up my scent in the sea so I hide here often. I would invite you to visit but it isn't very tidy." He swept out some shells and clumps of dried seaweed.

"Isn't it dangerous to sleep in here when the tide comes in?" Dory asked. "Doesn't the cave flood?"

Eli's muffled voice said, "The sea doesn't reach inside my hideaway."

"Then how did all those shells and seaweed get in there?"

Eli popped his head out of the opening. "Do not worry, Miss Dory. In all the time I have been here the tide has never come this high." He held out a little red velvet bag. "This bag contains our mother's jewellery," he said. "When Charlotte and I are together again I shall sell a few more pieces to pay for our passage to America and there I will make our fortune."

America. The pang in Dory's heart was so sharp it took her by surprise. She was stupid to think she could ever be a proper part of Eli's world. But he felt so real and so lovely.

"Are you all right, Miss Dory?" he asked.

"Yeah, it's just the air in here," Dory said. She focused on the red bag. "Aren't you worried someone will find that and steal it?"

"The villagers are afraid of this cave. They say hobgoblins live here," Eli said with a snort. "Besides, I have my treasure well hidden."

Dory looked at the red velvet bag again. "Where is your mother?" she asked.

Eli stepped back into the shadows. "In heaven."

"Sorry," Dory mumbled.

"Thank you." Eli climbed back out of the opening and dropped to the cave floor. "But Mama is always with me, advising me what to do," he said. "I know she wants me to be with Charlotte. It's her heart's desire."

Eli smiled at Dory with a strange brightness. His hair was like flame in the candlelight and she couldn't take her eyes off it. But then the candle sputtered, the cave's blackness closed in and a foul taste rose in her throat.

"Miss Dory!" Eli touched her arm.

"Got to get outside," Dory whispered.

Light bounced over the slimy walls as Eli helped her to the mouth of the cave, where Dory swallowed great mouthfuls of fresh air.

"Thanks," she said. "I'm all right now."

Below them, the sea swelled around the rocks and licked at the ledge of the cave.

"Hang on," Dory said. "This cave's going to flood any minute."

"There is nothing to worry about, Miss Dory." Eli helped her down from the ledge and they waded back towards the cove. By the time they reached the pebble beach, their clothes were wet and clinging to them and Dory's eyes stung with salt. Waves nipped at their feet as they hurried across the sand towards Scar Wood.

Eli veered right and made for a set of stone steps Dory had never seen before. They were half hidden behind shrubs. "This way, Miss Dory," he said. "There's no time to lose."

Dory hauled herself up as fast as she could with the pain in her knee. Halfway up, Eli took her hand and they climbed together. All Dory's pain dropped away at the feel of his warm hand in hers, but the pang in her heart returned.

At the top of the headland, they stole across the fields where Dory had met the hunters with the dog. Now she gasped at what she saw beyond the fields. A tall stone house with peaked roofs and towering chimneys stood at the top of Crake Ridge. It had a beautiful garden around it, sloping down to the cliff.

Dory realised with a shiver that at some point between 1863 and her time, this house and the land under it must have crumbled into the sea.

"Cliff House," Eli said in a sombre voice. "Charlotte's prison."

Dory squinted at the rows of windows. "There must be loads of rooms," she said. "How will I ever find her if I manage to get in?"

Eli slid a battered piece of paper from his jacket and unfolded it. "I drew a map of the house from memory," he said. He traced his finger over it. "Here is the pantry window I told you about. It will be easy for me to force it open. The back stairs lead to the nursery on the second floor and Charlotte's bedroom is beside it. The woman who watches her sleeps in this room just beyond Charlotte's own."

A shadow of doubt crossed Dory's mind. "So I go straight in, up those stairs and your sister is behind the second door," she said.

Eli put the map away. "Exactly."

"What if Charlotte screams when she sees me?" Dory asked.

"She won't," Eli said. "She has always been very brave and sensible for her age. But there is one problem. My father sits up late in his study and the servants don't go to bed until he does. You will have to go inside after everyone is asleep and it is still dark outside – no earlier than 2 o'clock and no later than 4."

Dory's heart sank. Could she get out of the B&B in the middle of the night without waking anyone? She and Gracie slept in the same room!

Eli moved closer. "I am so grateful for your help, Miss Dory."

Dory nodded but her mouth had gone dry. "What do I tell Charlotte when I see her?" she asked.

Eli inched a bit closer and Dory could see flecks of gold in his pupils. "I've been thinking," he said. "Would you bring Charlotte to meet me?"

Dory could barely breathe.

Eli leaned in, brushed her ear with his lips and murmured, "Would you bring her to my cave, Miss Dory? Please. I will wait for you there."

A thrill ran down Dory's back and she closed her eyes. "But how do I convince her to come with me?" she murmured. "I'm a stranger ..."

Eli took her hand. "Charlotte will trust you when she sees this." He took something out of his pocket and pressed it into her palm. "For you, Miss Dory."

A black pendant in the shape of a heart lay in her hand. It was carved with roses and strung onto a velvet cord.

Dory's nerves gave way to delight. "This is amazing," she said. "Is it stone? It's so light."

"It's made from a piece of jet found on this very shore," Eli said.

"I love it, Eli." Dory ran her fingers over the roses. "Thank you."

"When Charlotte sees it, she'll know she can trust you." Eli's eyes locked with Dory's. "The pendant was our mother's. I know Mama wants you to have it."

CHAPTER 5

"I will be waiting here tonight." Eli handed Dory the letter-box jar and its cork stopper. "You will never know how much this means to me, Miss Dory."

"Please – just call me Dory," she said. Her hand strayed to the jet heart around her neck.

He said it softly. "Dory."

Dory smiled and pushed the cork into the jar. Eli's world faded and gave way to her time. She stood for a moment by the tree while her heart throbbed with excitement. Dory's mind was in control again, telling her she would be daft to return that night and put herself in danger to help Eli. They had no future together so what was the point of breaking her heart over him? She'd be better to stay away than to risk getting caught inside Cliff House.

As Dory trudged back to the village, she kept touching the pendant to make sure it was still around her neck. She was almost convinced it would vanish like the world it had come from. As the rooftops of the village came into view, she took it off and hid it in her trouser pocket. The jet heart was all she had of Eli. She tried not to picture him hiding alone until the hunters captured him and took him to the place he would never escape from.

Her heart ached for him. If only they had been born in the same time …

Dory rooted all the coins out of her purse and darted into a shop on the main street of the village. She had just enough to buy a couple of cheese rolls, a torch and a tube of antiseptic ointment. She held the plastic bag to her chest like a precious cargo.

Gracie sat outside the B&B sketching in her notebook. She slid her sunglasses down her nose and looked at Dory. "Did the aliens abduct you again?" she asked.

"Yeah, and they got me back at 4 o'clock, right on the dot." Dory hid the carrier bag by her side and hurried inside.

"What's in the bag?" Gracie called.

Dory climbed upstairs and jammed her shopping behind a pile of spare blankets in the wardrobe.

Gracie appeared at the bedroom door with her arms crossed. "What are you up to?" she demanded.

Dory pulled off her damp top and launched it at her sister. "What does it look like? I'm getting changed."

"Dory!" Gracie batted the top away. "Yuck, that pongs. Did you roll about on dead fish?"

"I went looking for fossils," Dory said. "Got a bit wet."

Gracie's eyes narrowed. "Uh-huh. Since when were you interested in fossils?"

"Since now," said Dory. "I need a shower. Tell Mum and Dad I'm back."

"I'm not your servant." Gracie turned on her heel and yanked the bedroom door shut.

45

When she was sure she was alone, Dory slipped the jet pendant out of her trouser pocket and held it close. This secret treasure was hers, smuggled from the faraway past. No other girl had anything like it.

On the outing with her family, Dory admired the waterfall they visited like a good girl but her head was elsewhere. The black heart was back around her neck, hidden under a clean top and a long cotton scarf. The jet was so warm against her skin she could only just resist touching it. She imagined some handsome young man offering it to Eli's mum as a token of love. But what if Eli's terrible father had given it to her instead?

"You're very quiet, Dory," Dad said on the way back. "Is your knee bothering you?"

"It's OK," Dory said.

Gracie poked Dory's arm. "She just wants attention."

"Get off." Dory pushed her sister's hand away and addressed her parents. "Can we go to that Flynn guy's jewellery shop before it closes?"

"Yes, why not?" Dad said. "Have you got your piece of jet with you, Gracie?"

"Uh-huh." Gracie looked at Dory and said in a low voice, "I'm not stupid, you know."

Dory frowned. "No one said you were."

"I notice things." Gracie plugged her headphones into her ears and stared out of the window.

"And I've got no idea what you're on about," Dory said under her breath.

Flynn was busy at his workbench when they arrived at the shop, but he stepped out from behind the counter to welcome them. While Dad and Gracie chatted with him, Mum looked round the shop with Dory.

"See anything you like, love?" she asked. "If Gracie's getting a pendant, you can choose something too. How about some earrings?"

Dory had to put her hands in her pockets to keep them from going up to her own hidden pendant. "I don't really see anything I fancy, Mum," she said. "But thanks anyway."

Dory scanned the necklaces, brooches and earrings to see if she could find anything like the pendant. But they were all too modern. She was about to give up when she spotted an old display cabinet on the back wall with antique pieces inside. She studied the bead necklaces, cameos and lockets, but still there was nothing like her pendant.

"You ready to go, Dory?" Mum waited at the door. Dad and Gracie had already left the shop.

"Almost. You go ahead, Mum. I'll be out in one second." Dory hovered by the counter until Flynn looked up.

He smiled. "Anything else I can help you with?"

"Maybe," Dory said. "I saw this antique jet pendant shaped like a heart and carved with tiny roses. Have you got any like that?"

"No, I'm afraid not," Flynn said. "I wish I did. I could sell those ten times over."

"Do you know anything about them?" Dory asked.

"Well, there were a lot made in Queen Victoria's time," he said. "People wore loads of jet because of her. When her husband Prince Albert died, only jet jewellery was allowed at court."

"How come?" Dory asked.

"Because jet is black," Flynn said. "In those days, you had to wear black for a certain amount of time after a person died. The Queen wore nothing else, and ladies followed everything she did, so they wore jet too."

"So you'd wear a jet heart because someone had died?" Dory asked.

"That's right," said Flynn.

Dory shuddered. Eli's mother must have been mourning for someone when she wore it. So much for Dory's dreams of the heart as a romantic love token then.

Flynn gave her a funny look. "Are you OK?" he asked.

"Yes." Dory forced a smile. "Fine."

"Where did you see your antique heart?" Flynn asked.

"Uh, at another shop," she lied. "I can't remember where."

"There's a bit of a local legend about a jet heart that has turned up over the years," Flynn said. "Any time it turns up, strange things happen." He rubbed his thumb and fingers together as if he had a coin between them. "With a story like that, a piece of jewellery would be worth a fair bit!"

Dory tried to sound casual. "What strange things happen?" she asked.

"Oh, people said they saw odd things," he said. "And went to odd places that shouldn't exist."

Just as Dory was about to ask what he meant, Gracie pushed the shop door open. "Dad says to hurry up, Dory."

"I'm talking too much as usual." Flynn clapped his hands together. "I should close up shop."

Dory glared at her sister. "I'd better go then," she said. "Thank you."

Flynn gave her another odd look. "Bye, Dory."

"Bye." Dory stalked out of the shop. She wondered whether Flynn suspected she had the jet heart. He had given her such an strange look – it must have been written all over her stupid face. Maybe she'd better stop asking questions and steer clear or he'd work it out for sure.

Dory followed her family back to the B&B in silence.

CHAPTER 6

That night Dory set her phone alarm to vibrate and stashed it under her pillow. But she was so jumpy that she lay awake until well past midnight. Her knee itched under its bandage and she kept checking the time. In the end she lay still and pictured Eli's gorgeous face and at last that helped her fall asleep.

Dory woke in a panic at 3:30 a.m. Her phone had fallen between the bed and the wall, where it had hummed away but hadn't wakened her. She pulled her clothes on and slid the carrier bag of food and medicine out of the wardrobe. She prayed that Gracie would stay asleep as she opened the door and slipped out. She took the room key with her and left the main door of the B&B unlocked.

Once she was outside, Dory ran as fast as she could. The village houses were dark but she still stayed in the shadows and kept her torch beam low.

There was no dawn light yet, and the path to Crake Ridge was black and forbidding. A vixen's eerie shriek came from the fields and a moment later the animal crossed Dory's torch beam. Dory's insides turned over when it stopped and stared at her.

"Go away!" She waved her arms and the vixen darted out of the light. "Out of my way!" she yelled. "Anything out there, just stay away!"

By the time Dory reached the stone steps to Scar Wood, she was so on edge that she jumped at every crackle and screech. The ferns felt like fingers brushing her legs. Even the mossy tree became a looming monster in the dark. The night was alive with sounds.

Dory dug out the letter-box, and this time she wasn't surprised to see Charlotte's card inside it. She yanked out the cork stopper and called to Eli.

A short, hard laugh cut the darkness. "I'm here, Dory."

She let out a breath. "Eli, what a relief. I'm sorry I took so long!"

Dory's torch beam found him. He was chipping moss from the tree trunk. There was already a pile at his feet and he kept scraping as he spoke. "I wondered if you would come at all," he said, in a toneless voice. "I have been waiting a long time."

"I said I would." Dory smiled, hoping he would smile back. "Here I am, just a bit late."

But he didn't smile. He stopped scraping and put his hand up to shade his eyes from the light. "So you are, Dory," he said. "I thought you had changed your mind or become afraid."

"No," Dory said in the most convincing voice she could manage. "I'm not afraid." She held out the carrier bag. "I brought you some food. And ointment for your dog bite."

At last Eli smiled and she relaxed.

"Forgive me," he said, and his eyes went warm in that way that gave her butterflies. "I should not have doubted you." He swung down from his spot by the tree and picked moss from his fingernails. "You are an astonishing girl, Dory."

"I'm not," Dory said. She watched as he tore into the cheese rolls and studied the tube of ointment before smearing some on his leg.

"Thank you." Eli wiped his hand across his mouth. "We'd best go now. It will be dawn soon."

"Can I see your map again?" Dory asked. "The one of the house?"

"Of course. You should have it." He glanced at her neck and Dory pulled the jet heart out from under her shirt.

"I didn't forget this," Dory said. "It's the most beautiful thing anyone has ever given me." She swallowed back her questions about the person his mother had worn it to remember.

Eli's eyes shone. "You have one of these wonderful torches from your time," he said.

"You've seen them before?" Dory asked, and handed it to him to examine.

"Yes," he said. "Other visitors had them."

Dory raised her eyebrows. "So they came at night too?"

"Now and then," he said. "May I use the torch? Take my hand." He led her at speed through the woods and up the steps towards Cliff House. With each step, Dory's heart pounded harder at what lay ahead. It didn't help that Eli's grasp of her hand seemed cooler and more business-like than before.

At the top of the steps, Dory pulled on his sleeve. "Wait, where will the dog be?" she asked.

"It is chained near the gatekeeper's hut," he said. His hand glowed red as he covered the beam of the torch.

A stiff breeze blew in from the sea and Dory shivered as they crossed the fields and gardens to the great house. It was a black shape against the dark sky. Soon Dory would be alone inside, taking the biggest risk of her life.

Eli switched off the torch. "This way."

They ran round the silent house towards the servants' door at the back. A low whine came from a place not far away.

"Shhh." Eli grabbed Dory's hand so hard she winced. "The dog," he whispered. "We cannot let it hear us or it will wake the house with its barks."

Dory flinched at every whine. By the time they reached the pantry window, her bravery had seeped away. Had she lost her mind?

"What if they catch me inside?" she whispered. "What do they do to trespassers?"

"Are you about to desert me, Dory?" Eli hissed. "After you offered to help?"

"I don't want to but –" she began.

"But what?" Eli didn't sound angry now. There was a despairing note in his voice and it pricked at Dory's heart.

"Nothing," she said. "You're right. This was my idea." She chewed hard on her lip. "Show me how to get in."

"All right," he said. "Then I must leave you."

Eli forced the window open. Then he boosted Dory onto the sill and she wiggled through the small opening onto a stone sink inside. Eli handed her the torch and map of the house. "I am relying on you, Dory," he said. He touched her cheek once and vanished into the night.

Dory took a deep, shaky breath and listened to the wind whistling around the walls of the house. Then she tip-toed through the shadowy rooms and found the back stairs. With her heart in her mouth, she climbed to the second floor. A dark corridor loomed ahead with closed doors on each side.

Dory checked the map again and crept to the second door on the left. That was the one Eli had said was Charlotte's, wasn't it? She turned the handle and opened it. Her torch beam fell on a china doll on a chair by the fireplace, then the glint of a brass bed and a girl sleeping under a quilt. Her long red hair fanned out over the pillow.

Dory shut the door and crouched down near the bed. "Charlotte," she said under her breath. "Charlotte, please wake up."

The girl stirred and opened her eyes to slits. Dory aimed the torch at the floor and put her finger to her lips. "Don't be afraid!" she said. "I won't hurt you. Please don't make a sound. My name is Dory. I just want to talk to you."

Charlotte's eyes widened with fear. "Stay away or I shall scream," she said. She lifted her arm to protect herself.

Dory's heart thundered in her chest. "Shh, please don't," she begged. "I know I look strange. I come from far away but I don't mean you any harm. I've got good news, Charlotte. Your brother Eli is here. I'm to take you to meet him right now."

Charlotte's face twisted with terror and confusion. The wind shrieked at the windows as she whispered, "That is not possible. My brother is dead."

CHAPTER 7

Dory's jaw dropped. "That can't be right," she said. "I was just with Eli ..."

"You're making it up." Charlotte shook her head. "Eli died of fever at his school two years ago. He is buried in our graveyard."

An icy sliver of horror ran down Dory's spine. "But he's as alive as you and me. He told me all about you and your father and this house. He ran away from school so he could see you."

Charlotte squeezed her eyes shut. "You're lying. Why have you come to hurt me?"

"I'll prove I'm not lying!" Dory pulled the black heart pendant from under her top and held it up. "Eli said you would recognise this and know I'm telling the truth."

Charlotte let out a muffled cry. "Where did you get that?"

"From Eli," Dory said. "He said it belonged to your mother."

"A thief stole it from this house with all the rest of Mama's jewellery," Charlotte said. "My father's men are hunting him." She stopped and gave Dory a hard look. "And now you have it …"

"No, Eli gave it to me!" Dory let the heart drop to her chest as if it were hot. "He has the jewellery. I thought he'd inherited it but he must have taken it."

"You are making this up," Charlotte repeated. "How could my brother take the jewellery my mother wore because he had died?"

A wave of horror swept over Dory. "Eli can't be dead. He even showed me the message you put in the letter-box jar for him. He cried over it."

Charlotte's face softened. "You know about the letter-box?"

"Yes," said Dory. "He said you used to leave messages in it as a game. Doesn't that prove I'm telling the truth?"

"Perhaps," Charlotte said. "But I have not left a card in it since before Eli went to school."

"He said he told you to take care of the letter-box," Dory said. "Please listen to me, Charlotte. Your brother is alive and I've seen him. You look so much alike! You have the same lovely hair."

Tears gathered in Charlotte's eyes. "People do say the thief was a boy with red hair," she murmured, almost to herself.

"That's even more proof," Dory said, sensing she might be getting through to the girl. "But Eli's not a thief. He misses you, Charlotte. All he wants is to see you."

Charlotte's head dropped. "I would give anything to see him again," she said. "Eli was dearer to me than I can say."

"You can see him," Dory told her. "Right now."

But when Charlotte looked up again, her face was pinched. "If Eli is alive why did he not come himself?" she demanded.

"The only way in is through the pantry window – and he can't fit through it. Besides, it's too dangerous for him to come here again," Dory said. "Your father and his men are hunting for Eli so they can lock him away in school again.

"My father?" Tears rolled down Charlotte's cheeks. "How can that be? Why would Papa say Eli is dead if he is alive? He would never do such a thing!"

"I don't know." Dory's shoulders sagged. "I'm sorry."

The rising wind shook the glass in the windows and startled her. Silvery dawn light showed at the crack in the curtains.

"I have to go," Dory said. "Find Eli for yourself if you won't come with me. He hides in the cave under the cliff." As she took hold of the door handle, she added, "But please don't tell your father. If he catches Eli you'll never see him again."

"Wait." Charlotte wiped her face and jumped out of bed. "Do you promise me on your life that you are telling the truth?"

"On my life. Look, Charlotte, I took a massive risk coming here. And now I've got to go!"

"Show me where Eli is," Charlotte said. "Help me dress!"

Dory's hands shook with relief and nerves as she helped Charlotte into petticoats, a flouncy dress and ankle boots with buttons up the sides.

"We must go," Dory said. "Don't make a sound!"

Charlotte covered her head with a shawl and they tip-toed out of the bedroom. The wind battered at the house and drowned out the squeaks of the floorboards and steps as they made their way downstairs.

On the ground floor Dory whispered, "How on earth will you get through the pantry window in that dress?"

Charlotte scurried into the kitchen and took a heavy key from a pot on the table. "Cook always leaves it here," she said.

They unlocked the servants' door and dashed out into a stormy grey dawn. Dory helped Charlotte across the garden and through the fields, always listening for the dog. The gusts off the sea nearly blew them over, but she didn't care. She'd got Eli's sister out of Cliff House and she wanted to punch the air in triumph.

"Almost there," Dory said. "Just down the steps and along the beach."

Charlotte tried to keep her shawl from blowing away. "I will not believe it until I see Eli."

"Not long to go, Charlotte." The jet heart flew up into Dory's face and she jammed it under her shirt.

The wind pelted them with rain as Dory helped Charlotte down the steps and they struggled towards the pebble beach and rocks that marked the way to the cliff and Eli's cave.

Dory frowned at the incoming tide. "We have to get across those rocks, Charlotte," she said. "I'll help you as much as I can. Do you understand?"

"Yes." Charlotte gave her a tight smile. "I am ready."

They picked their way through tidal pools and over the rocks. The dawn light was growing weaker, not stronger. A curtain of black sky moved over the horizon and pushed the sea into churning white-capped breakers.

Dory boosted Charlotte onto the ledge of Eli's cave and hoisted herself up.

"This is it," she said, and squeezed Charlotte's arm. "He's inside."

Charlotte shook her wet skirt and hugged her shawl close. Her eyes were shining. "I cannot wait one moment longer."

Dory flicked on her torch and helped Charlotte into the void.

CHAPTER 8

The wind's howls grew fainter deep inside the cave. Dory's torch cut a bright circle out of the dark.

"Eli!" she called. "We're here! I have Charlotte."

Something thudded on the ground before them. Dory jerked the light onto the wall. Eli stood white-faced and silent beneath the hole he used as a sleeping place. His mouth opened but he was unable to speak.

Charlotte burst into tears. Eli stumbled forwards and folded her into his arms. Their heads fell together and their hair shone the same fire-bright colour.

"We did it," Dory said, but her voice trailed off. She smiled, trying to share their joy, but neither of them even looked at her.

Charlotte buried her face in Eli's chest. "I thought you were dead," she mumbled. "That you had a fever."

"I did have a fever." Eli stroked her back. "But I survived."

Charlotte's body shook. "Mama died of a broken heart for nothing."

"It is all Papa's fault!" Eli cried out. "If he had not sent me away ..."

Dory barely breathed as she held the shaky light on them.

"But where have you been all this time?" Charlotte sobbed.

Eli wiped his eyes with his sleeve but his face was stony. "Hidden away," he said. "But at last I found a way to escape. I walked for weeks so I could tell you the truth." At last he smiled down at his sister. "I shall never leave you again, Charlotte."

Then he turned his eyes to Dory, but they had none of their special warmth. "I cannot thank you enough, Dory," he said. "You have brought me the greatest gift."

"No problem," Dory said, her voice stiff. "But, Eli, we'd better go before the cave floods."

"Not yet," he said.

"Have you looked outside?" Dory asked. "It's blowing a gale! Don't worry, there's no one around to see us."

"They may be hunting for Charlotte by now," Eli said. He held his sister tight. "But they will never find us here."

Dory's temper flared. "Eli, we need to go!"

Eli ignored her. "Would you like to see where I've been sleeping, Charlotte?" he asked.

"I suppose so," his sister answered.

Dory's voice rose. "We don't have time for this."

Eli grabbed Charlotte by the waist and hoisted her up to the opening in the cave wall. "Climb in," he said.

"It's so dark," Charlotte complained. "And cold."

"Do not worry!" Eli laughed. "I will climb in after you and light a candle. We shall be snug and warm together." He gave her a swift push and she scrambled inside.

"It's too dangerous," Dory said. "There's a massive storm outside! I don't care what you say. The sea will flood this cave."

"We will stay," Eli said. "Nowhere else is safer."

Charlotte cried out from the shadowy hole. "Mama's velvet bag is here!"

"Yes," Eli said. "When I sell the jewels we will have money to go to America and make our fortune, Charlotte."

"But I don't want to go to America," Charlotte said. "May we go back to Cliff House instead, Eli? When Papa sees how well you are, we shall all live together again."

"No, Charlotte, Papa will never let me into his house," Eli answered. "We cannot live at Cliff House any more. Mama will be angry."

"But how could she be angry?" Charlotte wailed. "Mama is dead!"

"Mama is with us all the time." Eli held out his hand to Dory. "Come along, Dory, I will help you climb up with Charlotte. We'll wait there until the tide goes out."

Dory looked at him with fresh eyes. Her senses went on high alert now. "No way," she said. "I helped you but I have to go now. You weren't straight with me, Eli. Charlotte never wrote that card in the letter-box. And you took your own mother's jewellery from Cliff House."

"Mama's jewels belong to me and my sister," Eli said. "As for the card, I confess I did write it. Would you have helped me otherwise?" He stepped closer. "Come along, Dory, or the hunters will catch you and I cannot allow that."

Dory moved backwards over broken shells and seaweed. "No one is going to catch me. I'm going home, Eli."

"Come to America with us, Dory. We will have a wonderful new life." Eli's eyes began to shine in the warm way that had set Dory's heart racing before. But now it froze her inside.

"Not a chance!" she snapped. "You're putting Charlotte in danger. Let her go!"

Charlotte whimpered in the background, her face like a ghost's in the dark hole.

"Charlotte, jump down and I'll take you back," Dory called. She took a few more steps backwards. "Now!"

"Stay where you are, Charlotte," Eli said.

"Let us go, Eli!" his sister cried.

"Jump down!" Dory shouted. "You can do it, Charlotte!"

Eli lunged for Dory and she aimed the torch into his eyes. He flinched and in that split second, Dory turned and ran.

"Follow me, Charlotte!" she called. But she knew there was no way Eli would let his sister leave.

At the mouth of the cave the wind roared at Dory's ears and blew her hair into a tangle across her face. She dropped down off the ledge and struggled towards the pebble beach, battered by wind and spray.

"Dory!" Eli bellowed from the ledge.

"Get Charlotte and come now!" Dory shouted back.

"We cannot leave this cave." He shrank against the rock wall. "We belong here."

"What are you talking about?" Dory screamed.

"Goodbye, Dory."

As Dory turned away from him, the sea caught at her legs and swept her onto the pebbles. Scores of waves broke on the rocks with huge plumes of white water. As Dory scrambled to her feet, she heard a roar like thunder. A monster wave reared up and slammed straight into the cliff face, flooding Eli's cave. When that wave retreated, another thundered in behind and sucked two limp human shapes back out with it. They floated on the surface until the next wave swallowed them up and took them under.

Dory crawled up to the sand and curled into a ball. The wind whipped her clothes and chilled her skin, but she lay there crying until nothing was left inside her.

CHAPTER 9

Dory woke at the touch of Mum stroking her arm. She was back in her bed at the B&B.

"Dory love," Mum said, as she sat down on the side of the bed. "Breakfast is about to finish. You'd best get up if you want to eat."

"I'm not hungry." Dory's mouth still tasted of the bile she had thrown up after she saw Eli and Charlotte swept out to sea.

"Are you feeling all right, love?" Mum asked gently.

"My stomach was a bit off in the night," Dory mumbled. "It's OK now. I just want some sleep."

"OK then." Her mum stood up and pulled the curtains shut. "I'll wake you before we go for lunch."

Dory snuggled into the pillow and one hand crept up to feel around her neck. There was nothing there. She leaped out of bed in a panic and tore through her damp clothes until she found the heart pendant coiled up like a black viper in her trouser pocket. Dory couldn't recall putting it there, but then she didn't remember much after the wave hit the cave and she was sick. She must have stumbled back to the letter-box and closed it, then walked back to the B&B in a daze.

Dory sat down on the edge of the bath and looked at her things. They all looked strange, even her toothbrush and sun cream. These things belonged to a different Dory, an innocent one who hadn't crossed time and helped lure a girl to her death.

Dory couldn't bear to wear the jet heart so she stuffed it inside a sock in her suitcase and zipped the lid shut. Then she went back to bed until Mum made her get up. She sat in silence at lunch, eating nothing.

The only person quieter than Dory was Gracie. Her head was bent over her notebook as she doodled.

When lunch was over, Dad looked at his watch. "Gracie, your pendant should be ready," he said. "Let's head over to the jewellery shop."

Flynn nodded at them as soon as they entered.

"I was hoping you'd come in," he said, and he took a small box from a shelf. "Here it is, Gracie."

Gracie flipped the lid open and showed them all the pendant of polished jet. Mum helped her fasten it around her neck.

"It's fab," Gracie said, in a flat voice. "Thank you."

"My pleasure." Flynn grinned and turned to Dory. "Nothing here to tempt you, Dory? Only an antique heart will do, eh?"

"An antique heart?" Dad repeated. "Is that what you're after, love?"

Dory cringed. "Not really. I just thought they looked kind of cool."

"So have you seen any hobgoblins in the woods, Gracie?" Flynn asked.

Gracie fiddled with her new necklace. "No."

"Not yet," said Dad, and pulled two notes from his wallet. "But we have a few more days here so there's always a chance, eh, girls?"

"I want to ask Flynn something," Dory said as her parents drifted towards the door. "See you back at the B&B."

"I'll wait for you," said Gracie.

Dory gave her a warning glance. "Go with Mum and Dad. I'll catch you up."

Gracie tossed her head and stomped off.

"This isn't about hobgoblins, is it?" Flynn said to Dory. "You want to know more about jet hearts."

"That's part of it," Dory said. "Have you ever heard of a place called Cliff House? It used to be up on Crake Ridge, I think."

"Yes, of course." Flynn's smile faded. "It was a grand house, they say, until the cliffs eroded so far that it collapsed into the sea. That was long before I was born."

"Was there ever a girl called Charlotte who lived there?" Dory asked. She felt sick just saying the name aloud. "A long time ago, in Queen Victoria's time?"

"Who told you about Charlotte?" Flynn asked. "Was it one of the old boys down by the harbour? They love scaring visitors with the legend of the lost girls."

"The lost girls?" Dory said.

"If you're not careful in Scar Wood, the ghost of a boy called Eli will trick you into helping him," Flynn told her. "The legend says he seems as alive as you or me. A fair number of girls are supposed to have fallen for him over the years. But if you go with Eli, you might never return."

Ghost. Dory's stomach turned over. She'd held a dead boy's hand and felt his breath on her skin.

"The real life story is terribly sad," said Flynn. "Eli was Charlotte's older brother. He was sent off to boarding school where he got very ill and died. Their mother died soon after, then Charlotte drowned. The father lost his whole family."

Dory turned away and fanned her face with her hand, but it was no good. The tears came anyway.

"Oh dear. I am sorry," Flynn said, offering Dory a grubby hankie.

"Don't worry!" Dory forced an embarrassed smile and wiped her face. "What am I like? One sad story and it's waterworks time," she said. "Tell me the rest of the story, Flynn."

Flynn didn't look too sure but he went on. "Oh, it's just a silly story. They say that Eli lured Charlotte into danger so she would die and her spirit would join him. She drowned, but her spirit slipped away from him. He was left alone, and so he haunts the woods looking for girls to lure away. He's doomed to relive the tragedy over and over until the curse is broken."

Dory's stomach twisted again. So the letter-box had sucked her and the lost girls into Eli's nightmare world. Now she knew why he wouldn't leave the cave or let Charlotte go.

Her voice trembled. "How can the curse be broken?"

"No idea," said Flynn. "Don't worry yourself about it."

"Do you know anyone who's ever met Eli?" Dory asked, wiping her nose and swallowing back the last of her tears.

Flynn hesitated for a moment. "Many years ago a girl from the village claimed she had. She disappeared not long after."

"What was her name?"

"Rachel," Flynn said. "They say she drowned and people leave flowers for her on the fence along Crake Ridge. But the last time anyone saw her she was going down the steps to Scar Wood."

CHAPTER 10

That night Dory tossed and turned, unable to get Eli out of her head. Her blood ran ice-cold at the thought that his ghost had reeled her in with his sad story, warm looks and the jet black heart.

She went over everything Eli had said about Rachel and others who had 'visited' him from the future. He said they'd gone 'where they belonged'. Dory had assumed that he meant they'd returned to their own times, but had they? Were Rachel and the others lost for ever somewhere in Eli's dreadful world?

And what about the creepy way he talked about his dead mother? No wonder, since he was dead himself. The thought of that nearly made Dory throw up all over again. The questions rolled round and round in her mind, never to be answered. Her only comfort came from Gracie's soft, regular breathing in the other bed. Dory breathed in time with her sister and at last she fell into a deep sleep.

Dory woke up from a bad dream at 4 a.m. To calm herself down, she listened again for Gracie's breaths. When she heard nothing, she switched her bedside light on. Gracie's bed was empty.

Dory noticed Gracie's notebook sticking out from under her pillow. Something was wedged between its pages. When Dory pulled it out, one of Gracie's fossils fell to the floor. But Dory didn't bother to pick it up. Instead she stared at the sketch her sister had drawn on the page – a sad-looking boy with a black heart pendant in his hand.

Stunned, Dory unzipped her suitcase and thrust her hand into the sock where she had hidden her pendant. It was still there.

She dressed quickly, stuffed the jet heart into her trouser pocket and searched for her torch. It was gone. Dory felt sick with dread as she dug out the mini torch on her house keys and sneaked out. Within minutes she was hurrying along the path to Crake Ridge. But no animal screeches or rustling branches scared her tonight – not when she faced the much greater fear that Eli had Gracie.

The letter-box jar lay open below the mossy tree, with the cork stopper beside it. The card was missing and Dory felt her heart beat fast.

"Gracie!" Dory kicked at the ferns in frustration. She didn't know what else to do, so she closed the jar and shoved it back in the soil. When she dug it up again, the faded card had reappeared inside.

Dory pulled the cork out again and the night air shimmered around her as she had prayed it would. The faded ink darkened on the card and she slipped back into Eli's world.

Once Dory had hidden the letter-box and its stopper in the ground again, she rushed towards the cove. She moved the thin beam of her mini torch across the swaying trees in case Eli was lurking there, but there was no one.

"Gracie, I'm coming!" she shouted. "Gracie!"

The wind whistled back. At the cove, Dory peered out at the dark clouds and choppy sea. It looked like she had walked straight into the same storm as yesterday. How long did she have to escape the killer wave this time? As far as she could tell, the rising tide was still a short way from Eli's cave, but she had no idea where her sister was.

"Gracie? Where are you?" Dory called, but her voice was lost in the gale. She hurried up the steps and squinted at Cliff House. At first, the mansion was still and dark, but then she saw a single lamp in an upstairs room. Another was lit downstairs and glided past several windows. A third light appeared outside and moved along the edge of the house.

'Something has gone wrong. They've woken the others up,' Dory thought. She raced down to the beach. As she scrambled over the pebbles and rocks at the bottom of the cliff, terror rose in her gut. But when she pictured Gracie trapped in the darkness with Eli, anger drove her forwards.

Dory climbed into the cave and held the mini torch high above her head. "Eli?" she called. "I know you're here, hiding in the dark!" She stamped on the shells and seaweed underfoot. "I felt so sorry for you when I met you. In some ways I still do. But that was before I knew what you are and why you're here."

Eli's voice came low out of the blackness. "What am I, Dory?"

Dory's skin went clammy. "They call you a ghost in the village." Her torch beam found Eli sitting with his back against the rock wall. The bluish light bleached his skin white. He made no move to get up.

"A ghost," he said. "Is that what you think I am?"

"I think you're a lost soul that got trapped here," Dory said. She felt sick at the sight of him. "I saw the waves flood this cave yesterday and pull your body out. But today you're alive. The same storm is about to hit again. And you'll 'drown' again." She looked at her watch. "You have less than ten minutes."

"Then you had better leave and save yourself," Eli said. "I do not even know why you are here."

"Yes, you do!" Dory cried. "You have my sister Gracie."

"No." Eli flipped one hand at the darkness around him. "I do not."

"You sucked her in with your story, just like me. Gracie!" Dory yelled. "Tell me you're in here! Charlotte, are you here?" She shook with anger. "I saw lights at Cliff House. They're hunting for Charlotte and my sister, aren't they? Gracie's doing your dirty work."

"I never forced you and I never forced Gracie," Eli said. "You were both happy to help. You both offered."

"Just like Miss Rachel," Dory said, and her voice was acid. "Was she happy to die?"

Eli stared at her from under his eyebrows. The light from her torch was so weak he didn't even blink. "The sea took her," he said.

Dory scowled. "Don't blame the sea for what you did!"

Eli pushed himself to his feet. He didn't take his gaze from her.

Dory turned and ran. The dull light of the cave's opening was just ahead but she heard the crunch of his feet behind her. She thought her heart would explode when Eli clamped his arms around her.

"Let me go!" she screamed, as her tiny torch went flying. She strained towards the cave opening but only got a few inches before he pulled her back.

"Don't leave me." His breath was hot against her ear. "I am always alone."

Dory let out an angry cry. She channelled all her fury against him and forced them closer to the cave's opening. They slammed into the rock wall and, as Eli held her there, she saw the white waves rushing towards them.

"Maybe you can stop this," Dory said through clenched teeth. "Maybe you can break the curse. You've got to try!"

"I don't know how," Eli croaked and relaxed his grip a little.

"Get rid of the letter-box!" Dory said. "Stop people finding it!"

"I cannot," he said.

Dory moved closer to the ledge. "Then let Charlotte go," she said. "Stop trying to get her back. And leave this cave!"

"I must stay here," Eli said. "I cannot escape my fate."

Dory stared at him. "Fine. But it's not my fate and it's not Gracie's!"

He gripped her harder. "It will be."

"No!" Dory's heart pounded in her ears. She knew the wave was coming. In less than five minutes she would become one of the lost girls of Scar Wood.

Just then, a blood-curdling shriek rang out over the wind. A torch beam zigzagged over them. Eli stumbled back as something knocked him over and pushed him to the cave opening. Dory struggled to get free but together they lost their footing and plunged over the ledge.

CHAPTER 11

Eli's head hit the rocks with a thud. He released Dory and she thrashed away from his body, gasping as waist-high waves broke around her.

"Dory! Are you OK?" Gracie jumped down from the ledge and beamed the torch in Dory's face.

"Yeah," Dory spluttered. "Let's get out of here!"

But there was Charlotte bent over Eli. His body rose and fell with the swirling tide. She struggled to turn him over. "Help me!" she begged. "We cannot leave him!"

"We have to, Charlotte!" Dory yelled back.

Gracie's mouth fell open. "But he'll die, Dory!"

"He's already dead," Dory said. "Come on!" She put out her hand. "You too, Charlotte."

"I shall stay." Charlotte clung to Eli with tears and rain streaming down her face.

"Not this time!" Dory said. "Gracie, get her other arm."

They hauled Charlotte away from her brother. She screamed and struggled to get free as they fought their way to the shore.

Dory shook her hard. "Stop it!" she shouted. "We're trying to help you!"

"I want Eli!" Charlotte wailed.

Gracie spat out seawater before she could speak. "You listen to my sister or you'll die, all right?"

Charlotte let out a pitiful cry but stopped resisting them.

"Faster!" Dory begged them. "There's a monster wave coming any second."

"Charlotte's father and his men are coming too." Gracie nodded up at lantern lights moving along Crake Ridge.

When the girls staggered onto the pebble beach, Dory yelled for them to get further away from the sea. They teetered as far as the sand and fell on their knees, panting. The sky went black and the wind scraped at their clothes and hair.

Dory pushed herself up and looked towards the cliff. To her astonishment, Eli had climbed onto the ledge outside his cave and stood staring out to sea.

Dory swallowed back bile as the deadly wave rose. It gathered height and power as it rolled towards the cave. "No ..." she cried.

Charlotte wobbled to her feet and screeched. "Eli!"

"Don't look." Gracie tackled her and hugged her tight. The wave smashed onto the ledge and dragged Eli away.

A dog howled from the steps to Cliff House.

"They've spotted us," Dory said. She dragged her sister away from Charlotte. "Come on, Gracie, leg it!"

They raced towards Scar Wood.

Men with lanterns were running towards Charlotte, but she got to her feet and ran away from them – back towards the sea.

"Will she be OK?" Gracie gasped.

"I don't know." Dory was panting so much she could barely speak. "She usually drowns and this time she didn't."

Gracie goggled at her. "How do you know that?"

"Yesterday I saw the same wave drown Eli and Charlotte." They had reached the mossy tree. Dory fell to her knees and dug out the letter-box jar. "This place is in some freaky time bubble," she said. "They keep repeating what happened here in 1863."

"But Charlotte's still alive." Gracie's teeth began to chatter.

"So it seems," said Dory. She stuffed the cork into the jar and grabbed her sister's hand.

Eli and Charlotte's world vanished and Dory nearly collapsed with relief at the pink morning light above the trees.

Dory held her sister close as she explained everything.

Gracie hugged her with shivering arms. "Thanks for coming after me," she said. "I was so scared. I didn't think we'd make it to the cave. I fell out of that pantry window and the dog barked. The whole house woke up. We had to run down to the beach and Charlotte was so slow."

Dory held her tight. "I should thank you for knocking Eli into the water."

"His face was so scary," Gracie said. "I thought he was going to kill you."

"He tried. If you hadn't turned up ..." Dory stroked her sister's wet hair and began to cry. "You do know I love you, right?"

"Yeah." Gracie grinned through her own tears. "I love you too."

"You drive me mad but I don't know what I'd do without you."

"Same for me," said Gracie. "I was so stupid. I shouldn't even have gone back to see Eli but I was under a spell or something." She went pink. "He gave me goose bumps he was so lovely."

"Me too – and he's not even real." Dory gave a shaky laugh. "He gives me goose bumps now, but not the kind you mean." She shook the card inside the jar. "How did you find out about this?"

Gracie looked sheepish. "When you went for your walk in the afternoon, I followed and saw how you disappeared. I came back in the morning while you were asleep and met Eli."

"How sneaky," Dory said.

Gracie made a face. "If you'd told me then I wouldn't have had to find out for myself."

"You're impossible, Gracie." Dory set off towards the stone steps with the glass jar in her hand. "Let's get out of here."

Gracie brushed off her clothes and followed. "Aren't you going to put that back?"

"No way," Dory snorted.

They climbed the stone steps and walked along the cliff path to the village. Dory scanned the fence as they walked.

She stopped short, puzzled, at the spot where the flowers had been. "Where's the posy gone?"

"Maybe somebody took it down," Gracie said.

"It was here when I came past before." Dory looked in the weeds on the ground and ran her hand along the wooden fence. "There's no sign of it. Not even a petal."

"Does it matter?" Gracie asked.

Dory frowned. "Yeah, it does. Those flowers were for a local girl called Rachel. She met Eli years ago and didn't come back. And I found out there were other lost girls like her." She placed the letter-box jar on the other side of the fence and climbed over. "You coming?"

Gracie looked scared but she followed her sister to the far edge of the cliff before the ground sheared away. A calm tide was coming in over the rocks below.

Dory held the letter-box in front of her as if it contained poison. "Ready to end this? So no one else can ever find Eli again?"

Gracie raised her fists in the air. "Go on!"

"Rest in peace, Rachel." Dory threw the glass jar as far as she could. It tumbled through the air and smashed into a thousand shards on the rocks below. The card fluttered out then sank into the water.

"Rest in peace all the lost girls," Gracie said. She turned to leave but Dory grabbed her hand and pushed her jet heart into the palm.

"Oh." Gracie shrank when she saw the pendant. "You got one too."

"Yeah," said Dory. "Come on, let's see yours."

Gracie screwed up her mouth and pulled her jet heart out from under her top. "It's the same."

"So much for being Eli's special girl, huh?" Dory snorted. "He gave us both the same gift. Did he tell you that his dead mama wanted you to have it?"

"Yuck! Yes." Gracie took the pendant off and dangled the cord from her fingers. "I don't even want to touch it now."

"Nor do I," Dory said. "We could sell them to Flynn for a wad of cash, you know."

Gracie shook her head. "I don't want anyone else to have this nasty thing, even for a ton of money."

Dory grinned. "Shall we give them back to the sea instead?"

Gracie took her sister's hand and together they flung the black hearts at the pink horizon.

CHAPTER 12

When Flynn's shop opened, Dory and Gracie were his first two customers.

"Good morning, girls," he said. "What can I do for you?"

"I was thinking of getting a pendant like Gracie's," Dory said. "Just a chunk of jet on a chain."

"Have a look at these." Flynn smiled and took a box from a shelf in his workshop. He poured a pile of jet pieces onto the counter. The girls raked through them and picked up a few to examine.

"So, Flynn," Gracie said. "We were walking along Crake Ridge and we spotted that the posy of flowers is gone."

"Flowers?" Flynn looked up.

"The memorial," Dory said. "The pink flowers."

Flynn furrowed his brow. "I don't know of anything like that on Crake Ridge."

"You said it was for a local girl called Rachel who drowned," Dory said.

"Sorry?" said Flynn. "We haven't had a drowning around here for years, thank goodness. And the only Rachel in this village is right there." He waved at a middle-aged woman outside the post office across the street.

Dory and Gracie stared at each other, mouths open.

"I don't understand," Dory said. "You told me there was a Rachel who was last seen going down the steps to Scar Wood ..."

Flynn looked confused. "I never said that, Dory."

"You talked about the legend of the lost girls." Dory's face flushed. "About the ghost of Eli and his curse."

"I'm sorry, you've lost me." Flynn stepped back and put his hands up. "Ghosts and curses? Lost girls?"

"Yes," Dory insisted. "I asked you about Cliff House and Charlotte, the girl that lived there in Queen Victoria's time."

"I remember that part," Flynn said. "Her brother Eli died of fever and their mother died soon after, then Charlotte drowned. Awful story."

"And Eli came back as a ghost in Scar Wood, right?" Gracie said.

Flynn shook his head and smiled. "Not that I ever heard. Only the hobgoblins haunt Scar Wood."

Dory's confusion grew. This was too weird. "So isn't there a local legend about Eli's ghost luring girls in?" she asked.

"No, but it sounds terrific," said Flynn. "We should spread it round the village. That would bring the tourists in."

Dory put down the chunks of jet. "I can't decide between these," she mumbled. "Can you put them aside and I'll come back later?"

"Sure," said Flynn. "By the way, Charlotte and Eli's graves are up in the churchyard."

Dory was startled. "I thought his grave was behind Cliff House," she said.

Flynn raised his eyebrows. "Yes, but the family's graves were moved before the house fell into the sea."

"Right." Dory exchanged a look with Gracie. "We should go."

"If you head up there, look for the tomb with the angel on it," Flynn called after them.

As they climbed the steep lane up to the church, Dory asked, "Am I crazy? Flynn acted like he didn't know any of the things he told me yesterday!"

"I believe you," Gracie said. "But I don't think Flynn was acting. He'd never heard of Eli's curse."

"And how could Rachel be alive?" Dory stopped and grabbed her sister's arm. "Unless it's because we stopped Eli last night when we destroyed the letter-box jar."

Gracie's mouth hung open. "You mean we broke the curse and brought Rachel back?"

"Have you got a better explanation?" Dory hurried up the lane with Gracie right behind her.

The graveyard beside the grey church was gloomy even in the sunshine. The girls wandered along the paths between the old graves until Gracie said, "Over there!"

A sad-faced stone angel stood in the furthest corner of the churchyard. Dory's heart beat faster as she approached it.

"Look," Gracie breathed, as she peered at one side of the plinth. "Beloved daughter Charlotte, born 26 April 1851, died 14 August 1863." She took Dory's hand and squeezed it. "I thought we saved her last night but she still drowned."

"I guess we couldn't change that." A rush of bleak sadness came over Dory as they walked around the gravestone. The next side said

'Beloved wife and mother', and the third was for Charlotte and Eli's father.

Dory knew what the fourth side would say but her heart still pounded as she turned the last corner.

"Beloved son, Eli, born 27 October 1844, died 7 February 1861," Gracie whispered. "His bones are right under us. Yuck."

A clammy breeze rustled the leaves behind them. The hairs stood up on Dory's bare arms. She whirled round and squinted at the tangle of trees and bushes.

Gracie put an arm around her shoulders. "What is it?"

"Nothing," Dory muttered. "I'm seeing things. Come on. Let's get out of here."

When they had gone just a few paces, Dory looked back again. She still saw nothing in the trees but her eye caught something else.

"Gracie," she said in a low voice. "The angel's hand."

"What about it? It's holding a rose."

"No, the other hand." Dory led her back towards the tomb. The statue's left hand was by its side but there was something in its fingers.

Dory heard Gracie's sharp intake of breath.

It was grey instead of black and it was carved into the angel's robe, but there it was – a stone heart decorated with carved roses, dangling from a cord.

A wave of sickness came over Dory. The ground rose and the sky went sideways. The next thing she knew Gracie was pulling her up and helping her stumble away.

"Don't look back," Gracie panted.

Dory tried not to look, but it was no use. Before they went out of the gate, she turned just in time to see Eli's grinning face among the leaves.

Our books are tested
for children and young people by
children and young people.

Thanks to everyone who consulted on
a manuscript for their time and effort in
helping us to make our books better
for our readers.